This book belongs to

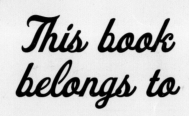

....

....

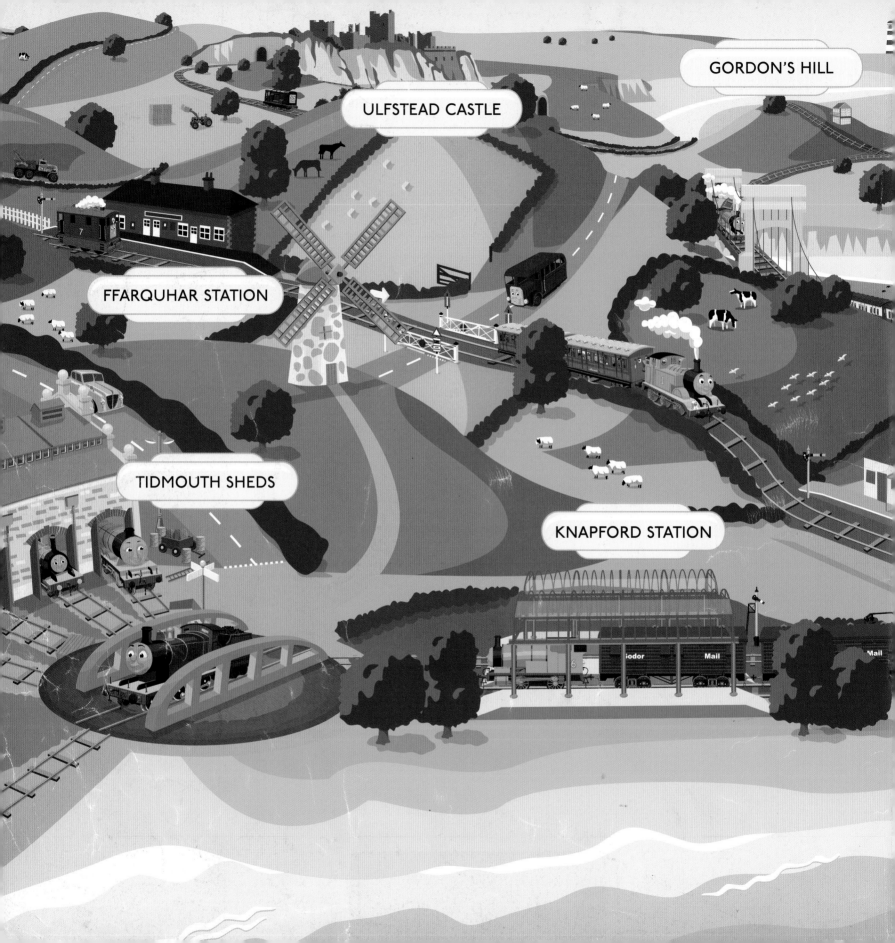

GORDON'S HILL

ULFSTEAD CASTLE

FFARQUHAR STATION

TIDMOUTH SHEDS

KNAPFORD STATION

BRENDAM DOCKS

CHINA CLAY PITS

DRYAW STATION

THE ISLAND of SODOR

EGMONT

We bring stories to life

Based on Thomas the Tank Engine first published in Great Britain in 1946
This edition published in 2015
by Egmont UK Limited
The Yellow Building, 1 Nicholas Road, London W11 4AN

Written by Ronne Randall
Illustrated by Robin Davies
Map illustration by Dan Crisp

Thomas the Tank Engine & Friends ™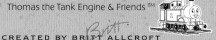

CREATED BY BRITT ALLCROFT

Based on the Railway Series by the Reverend W Awdry
© 2015 Gullane (Thomas) LLC. Thomas the Tank Engine & Friends and
Thomas & Friends are trademarks of Gullane (Thomas) Limited.
Thomas the Tank Engine & Friends and Design is Reg. U.S. Pat. & Tm. Off.
© 2015 HIT Entertainment Limited.

ISBN 978 1 4052 7604 7
59058/1

Printed in Italy

Stay safe online. Any website addresses listed in this book are correct
at the time of going to print. However, Egmont is not responsible for content
hosted by third parties. Please be aware that online content can be subject
to change and websites can contain content that is unsuitable for children.
We advise that all children are supervised when using the internet.

FSC
www.fsc.org

MIX
Paper from
responsible sources
FSC® C018306

Egmont is passionate about helping to preserve the
world's remaining ancient forests. We only use paper
from legal and sustainable forest sources.

This book is made from paper certified by the Forest
Stewardship Council® (FSC®), an organisation dedicated to
promoting responsible management of forest resources.
For more information on the FSC, please visit www.fsc.org.
To learn more about Egmont's sustainable paper policy,
please visit www.egmont.co.uk/ethical

THE STORY OF

Thomas
the Tank Engine

This is a story about Thomas the Tank Engine, who worked with his engine friends on The Fat Controller's Railway on the Island of Sodor.

Thomas the Tank Engine was a cheeky little engine who helped the big engines by pulling their coaches to and from the **BIG** Station.

But what Thomas really wanted was his very own Branch Line. That way he would be a **Really Useful Engine.**

Sometimes Thomas liked to play tricks on the other engines.

One day, when Gordon, the **BIG STRONG** engine, was very tired from pulling the heavy Express train, Thomas came up beside him and whistled loudly.

"PEEP! PEEP!

WAKE UP, LAZYBONES!"

That gave Gordon a fright! He decided to teach cheeky Thomas a lesson.

The next morning, Thomas would
not wake up. It was nearly time
for Gordon's Express to leave,
and Thomas hadn't got his
coaches ready.

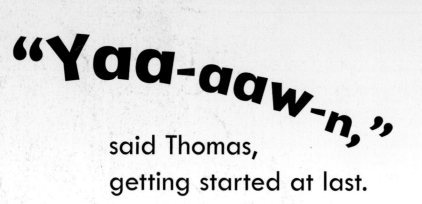

"Yaa-aaw-n,"
said Thomas,
getting started at last.

"Hurry up, Thomas!"
said Gordon crossly.

Thomas' job was to push Gordon's train to help him start.

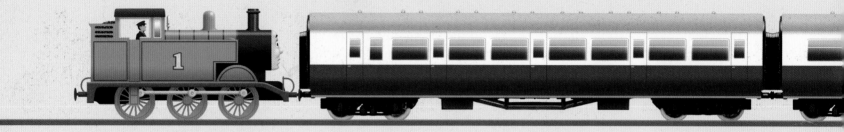

As he moved out of the station, he started to go *faster* and **faster**.

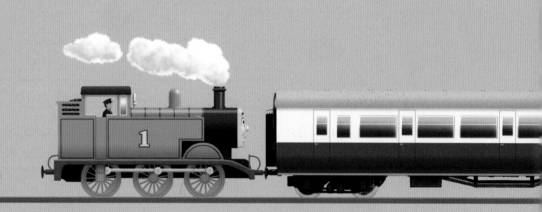

Faster and **faster** and **faster** and **faster** went Gordon.

It was much too **fast** for Thomas!

That morning was Gordon's chance to teach Thomas a lesson.

"Hurry, hurry, hurry, hurry!"
laughed Gordon.

Poor Thomas was going **_faster_**
than he had ever gone before.

"My wheels will wear out!"

he thought.

"**Peep!** Peep!

Stop! Stop!"

whistled Thomas.

At last they stopped at a station.

"Well, Thomas," chuckled Gordon.
"Now you know how it feels
to be tricked!"

"Puff!
Puff!"

panted poor Thomas.

He was too out of breath to say anything.
His cheekiness had got him into trouble.
Perhaps he would never get his
own Branch Line now.

The next day, Thomas saw some strange-looking trucks in the Yard.

"That's the breakdown train," said his Driver. "It helps out when there's an accident."

Just then, James, the Splendid Red Engine, came through the Yard crying.

His trucks were pushing him too **fast**, and his brake blocks were on fire!

"HELP! HELP!"

Soon after James disappeared, a man came running.

"James is off the line! We need the breakdown train – quickly!" he shouted.

Thomas was coupled on to the breakdown train, and off he went as **fast** as he could.

Whirrrrr went his wheels along the track.

"I must help James," he said.

They found James in a field, with the trucks piled in a heap behind him. His Driver and Fireman were checking that he was all right.

"It wasn't your fault, James," his Driver said.
"It was those Troublesome Trucks!"

James needed help. Thomas
pushed the breakdown train
alongside James.

Then he pulled some trucks
out of the way.

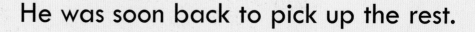

He was soon back to pick up the rest.

"Oh... dear!
Oh... dear!"
they groaned.

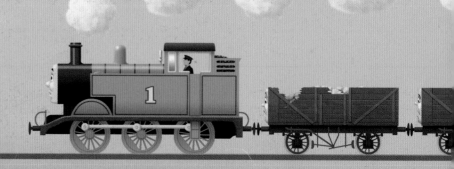

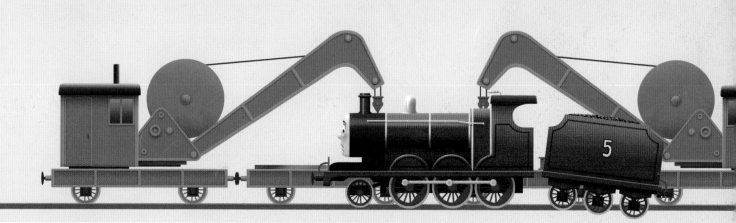

"Serves you right. Serves you right," puffed Thomas crossly. He worked hard all afternoon.

Thomas pulled James back to the Shed, where The Fat Controller was waiting.

"Well, Thomas," he said, "you have shown that you're a **Really Useful Engine**. I'm so pleased with you that I'm going to give you your own Branch Line."

"Oh, thank you, Sir!"
said Thomas happily.

Now Thomas is happy as can be, and he **chuffs** and **puffs** proudly along his own Branch Line from morning till night.

Gordon is always in a hurry, but whenever he sees Thomas he remembers to say, **"Hurry! Hurry!"** And cheeky little Thomas always whistles,

"PEEP! PEEP!

Lazybones!"

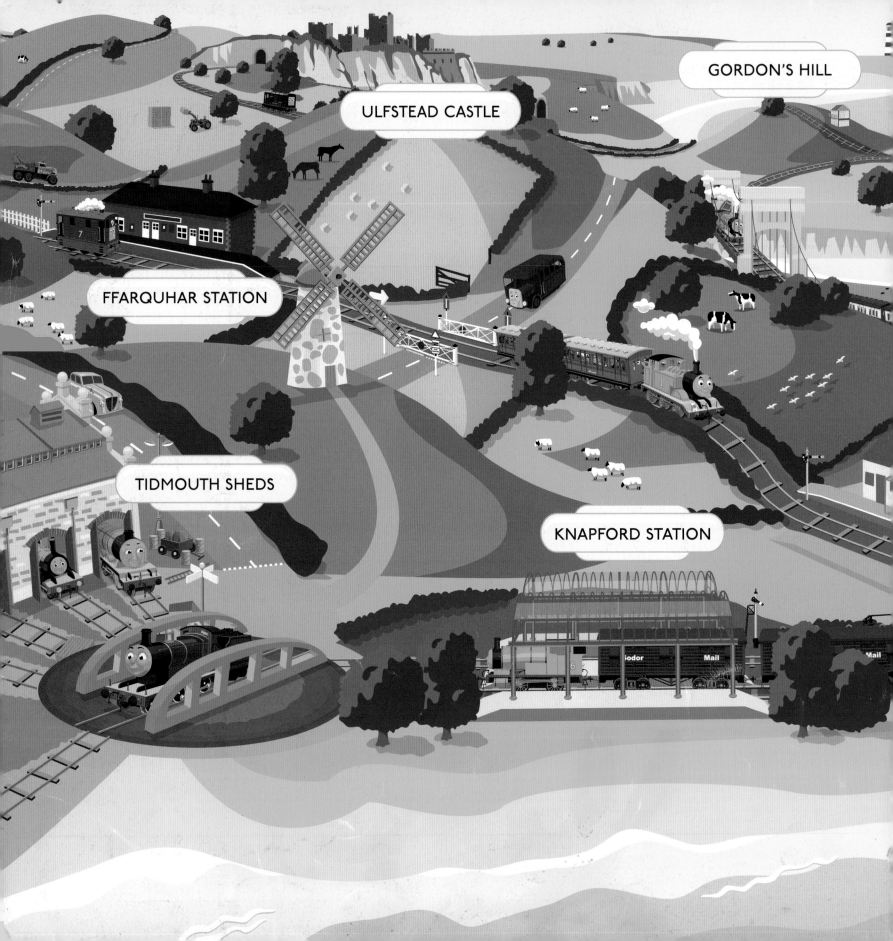

GORDON'S HILL

ULFSTEAD CASTLE

FFARQUHAR STATION

TIDMOUTH SHEDS

KNAPFORD STATION

CHINA CLAY PITS

BRENDAM DOCKS

DRYAW STATION

THE ISLAND of SODOR

About the author

The Reverend W. Awdry was the creator of 26 little books about Thomas and his famous engine friends, the first being published in 1945. The stories came about when the Reverend's two-year-old son Christopher was ill in bed with the measles. Awdry invented stories to amuse him, which Christopher then asked to hear time and time again. And now for 70 years, children all around the world have been asking to hear these stories about Thomas, Edward, Gordon, James and the many other Really Useful Engines.

The Three Railway Engines, first published in 1945.

The Reverend Awdry with some of his readers at a model railway exhibition.

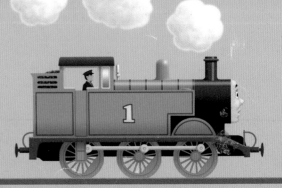